CAESAR'S
CAPTAIN

THROUGH MY EYES| CHRISTIAN HISTORICAL FICTION| BIBLICAL FICTION

Abby B Rob

Table of Contents

About the Author

My name is Abby Robertson. I am a devout Christian, wife and friend. I never have considered myself a writer due to my inabilities (extreme dyslexia, mediocre writing ability, and lack of eloquent words) but, by a work of God this book was written. This message was placed on my heart so others can see Jesus the way I know him.

"God, my shepherd! I don't need a thing. You have bedded me down in lush meadows, you find me quiet pools to drink from. True to your word, you let me catch my breath and send me in the right direction. Even when the way goes through Death Valley, I'm not afraid when you walk at my side. Your trusty shepherd's crook makes me feel secure. You serve me a six-course dinner right in front of my enemies. You revive my drooping head; my cup brims with blessing. Your beauty and love chase after me every day of my life. I'm back home in the house of God for the rest of my life."

Psalms 23 MSG

I wanted to write a Christian fiction book that helps others see Christ the right way. A friend, a counselor, a healer and kind. Also to bring a realistic story with raw emotions and real life experiences with scripture passages. Some of you may not know but, the bible has some wild not G rated stories. It amazes me how God uses not the strongest, perfect or best suited people but the one who are willing to be in relationship with him and give him glory. He uses messy, imperfect humans to accomplish his master plan.

So many individuals have the wrong perspective of Christianity due to rejection from so-called self-righteous "Christians", a Church or a pastor. It breaks my heart how so many distort the bible for their own personal agenda. That is not what it is intended for and leaves many individuals with spiritual trauma. The bible clearly states…

"There is therefore now no condemnation for those

who are in Christ Jesus. 2For the law of the Spirit of life has set you free in Christ Jesus from the law of sin and death"

Romans 8 : 1-2 ESV

It is my greatest passion to relight Jesus and the bible in

6

a way that others can heal and understand God's true character. GOD IS LOVE. God desires to have a relationship with you and give you the best. He will meet you wherever you are in life. No matter if you're broken, depressed, angry, addicted, bitter, anxious, overwhelmed, (you name it), he still loves you. He wants to love you and help you to a free life, you simply have to ask him.

"Those who are loved by God, let his love continually pour from you to one another, because God is love"

1 John 4 : 7 TPT

Chapter One

Lucius choked back his wine. Dust hung in the air of the small tavern hidden in a dark alley in Jerusalem. Several of the soldiers who reported to him sat across the dimly lit space, carrying on about who was stronger and who got more women. Lucius listened intently, but he preferred to maintain his distance from such talk; however, as captain, he needed to be aware of the soldiers' activities within the city. His affection, however, secretly belonged to Valencia Anatolia, daughter of Cicero Anatolia Amata, a high-ranking official in Pilate's government. Lucius would have already asked for her hand in marriage if it weren't for Roman law forbidding marriage for soldiers in its ranks and his secret heritage. That fact saddened him. He didn't like to sulk on indefinite facts, but this week had been extremely grueling for him, and he was buzzed.

He picked up his glass and swirled the burgundy liquid around, the glass's copper color causing the wine to appear sour. Wine wasn't his preference, but it did help him relax and forget his day's troubles—troubles that followed him and haunted his dreams no matter what stress his daily circumstances brought. He sipped the wine again and let out a soft sigh as he heard a snicker from an approaching guard: Sebastian Decimus, not a friend, but at least an amiable soldier to speak with.

"Captain, you hear what's been happening lately?" Sebastian spoke firmly and nudged Lucius with his elbow as he slunk onto the barstool next to him. He gestured for the barkeep to come. The man's shaggy brown curls mirrored his own, and he wondered if he looked as awkward. Lucius gave him the side-eye and turned back to his wine, tilting the cup from side to side. He'd been too absorbed in his soul-searching and full work week to pay attention to the rest of the world. Luicis focused all his energy towards keeping Jerusalem at peace, so he hardly knew what went on in the outer provinces. He shrugged and downed the rest of his wine, setting the glass on the bar as the keep approached.

"You boys having another?" The barkeep's gruff voice grated on Lucius already frazzled nerves.

"One more." Lucius slid a copper across the bar and forced a smile, and the keeper took his glass and retreated.

"This Nazarene Jew is causing quite a stir among the Jewish religious leaders. Consequently, he arrived here the day before last and the chaos is

centering in on the city—and with their holiday
Pesach (pay-sockh) is approaching. You know the
Passover always brings crowds of record sizes."
Out of the corner of his eye, Lucius saw Sebastion
shake his head. The man's face looked darker than
normal as if the week of peacekeeping in the
streets had darkened it, and he wondered if his
olive skin looked as sun-kissed.

"Why should I care?" Lucuis asked,
confused. Romans rarely got involved in Jewish
laws and customs. They were just there to keep the
peace, collect Ceasar's taxes, and keep Roman
control of Israel.

"Well, this is your command to keep
watch, and if that Jew creates a stir in the city,
your head will roll when we don't keep it
contained."

"I am your captain. Watch your tone with
me."
Sebastian was a little too casual and disrespectful
for Lucius' liking. He was younger, slightly
arrogant, but a good soldier. Lucius respected him
at least. Sebastion was right. With only two
centuria in Jerusalem, he would be held
accountable for keeping the peace. Just another
problem weighing him down. His thoughts
wandered to events that had happened a few weeks
prior, how he'd been forced to intervene in a

domestic squabble between two Roman citizens who'd accompanied Herod as he came to town for diplomatic conversations with the governor. How men could cause uproars and be so petty was beyond him. There had to be more to life than being *right* or *powerful.* But as it seemed, all men lusted after was to be right and powerful—at least all the men he had met thus far.

Lucius needed all the facts since it was his duty to be in the know. "What is his name?"

"Jesus." Sebastian paused slightly. He looked down, thinking intently, and said, "They say he raised the dead- several, in fact."

The words out of Sebastian's mouth intrigued Lucius, and he turned on his stool to look at him more carefully, resting his elbow on the bar. Sebastian was not known for hearsay. Still, the claim was extravagant. A man giving life was unheard of. If this were true, Caesar himself would be shaking his hand, asking how he did it. But rumors were just rumors, and Caesar surely had not paid any mind to this Jesus fellow.

"Raised the dead?" Lucius raised his brow.

"Yes, as well as many other troubling reports. A man, Simon, was a leper, and now he isn't. Healed from head to toe. Blind seeing, the deaf hearing, lame walking."

The barkeep slid two copper-colored glasses of dark liquid in front of the men and listened as Sebastian continued.

"The Jewish religious leaders absolutely hate him." Sebastian lowering his voice to a whisper. "They are out for blood. I have a feeling trouble is bound to happen, Captain." Lucuis pushed back his brown wavy hair and rolled his eyes in frustration. Why couldn't his job be easier, he thought.

"You talking about that Jew? The one from the middle of nowhere? The Nazarene?" The barkeep, Titus, eavesdropping on their conversation, retrieved the coppers from the bar in front of them, sliding them into a leather pouch tied on his belt. Being the barkeep to the most discreet pub in the city, he overheard and saw plenty of questionable exchanges.

"Yeah. Jesus, the Nazarene." Sebastian nodded.

"You know what I heard?" The barkeep leaned in close bringing his voice to a whisper. "I heard the teacher was at the Mount of Olives, and those from the Sanhedrin approached him bringing a woman, caught in the very act of adultery. Didn't even give the poor girl time to dress for what should have been her funeral. They threw her down in front of him and asked his guidance on what to do with her, all the crowd and leaders involved all knowing the law was immediately stoning. The teacher said he forgave her and told her to not sin anymore. Can you believe it?" he scoffed. "He is crazy. The Jews will still be coming for him."

The words made Lucius chuckle. "A Jew? Going against their law's condemnation?" The Jews were unforgiving and showed no mercy when it came to their extensive laws. Rome rarely got involved in the brutal customs of the Jewish religious leaders, favoring to work in tandem with them and give them space to keep them contained. However, stoning seemed to be the punishment— and death—of choice for breaking even one law. At least one or two happened every few months. Lucius had often wondered why the religious laws were so rigid and strict, though Roman law wasn't much better.

"Yes. Jewish law says the woman should have been stoned on the spot. The men there gathered around would have, except the teacher said the most baffling thing to them. He said, 'Whoever is without sin cast the first stone.' That is either crazy or straight from the gods, in my opinion. Then one by one, each of the men dropped their stones, oldest first." The barkeep tapped the bar in front of Lucius. "But mark my words, there will be trouble in Jerusalem if that man stays."

Lucius rolled his eyes and turned back to his wine. The last thing he wanted was more trouble. Day in and day out, it seemed they dealt with angry citizens, uprisings among merchants in the city, even reminders to pray to Jupiter for the protection of the state. There had to be more to life than warring and strife and men trying to outdo one another.

"May Bacchus, god of wine and ecstasy, bless your drink," the barkeep said before walking away, a common phrase heard in every dark alley tavern in the city.

"What do you make of it?" Sebastian said, staring off at the barkeep, pondering his words as he gulped down his wine. Lucius took his own but only studied the burgundy hue of the tart drink. He didn't know what to make of it. It could be that the man was nothing more than a philanthropist, encouraging those who practiced his religion. Or it could be that he was a revolutionary, just upsetting the Jewish religious leaders. Either way, for all Lucius cared, Jesus of Nazareth was a speck of dust in his eye, a pest in keeping peace in the city.

Any man who goes about supposedly healing the sick and saving people from a stoning was not a dangerous man they need to worry about. The Jews should be thankful for a man healing the sick and leave Rome out of it.

"I think you should mind your own business, Sebastian. We have enough to deal with having extra dignitaries in town and at the time of Passover."

"They call it Pesach. Like, what does that mean, anyway? And why travel to Jerusalem to give away your lambs and money?"

"I'm not a Jew, so I call it Passover." Lucius was amused by Sebastian. "Listen, unless he causes problems, we should focus on making sure the week's end goes smoothly and the religious people have their little holiday, all right?"

The answer seemed to appease Sebastian who rose, drinks in hand. Lucius was grateful for the reprieve and gulped down his wine; he too stood and left. The night air was cool on his skin as he slipped into the alley and turned toward the barracks. He longed for the taste of Valencia's lips, to feel her arms comfort him after his hard day.

He shuffled over the cobblestone in the dark, one foot in front of the other, until he was home. Opening the door, he let himself in and began removing his armor. Val was waiting for him—she was his favorite pastime.

Chapter Two

Lucius's breath came heavy and hard as he collapsed onto the bed. Valencia curled up next to him, her body damps with sweat after their little encounter. It seemed to be happening too often to go unnoticed by the servants. If discovered, she would be disowned by her family, and Lucius would be fairly beaten and have to pay heavy compensation for her virginity. She smelled of the rose water in which she bathed, her creamy skin soft against his. Sating his body with lust at least took the edge off, and he was thankful to have Val here now, even if it wasn't the forever he wanted with her. Others under his command would visit the brothels at the baths which Lucius found to be distasteful. Secretly, he was a hopeless romantic, though he was too much of a man to admit it to anyone. He wanted the best for her, even though he knew he could not give it to her.

"What are you thinking?" Val swirled her finger in the dark hair on Lucius' chest, gazing up at him with her large brown eyes. Her auburn hair, dampened with sweat, clung in small ringlets around her forehead and neck and lay across his shoulder. He brushed a few of the strands back from her eyes and forced a smile.

"I was thinking of my mother." He was the illegitimate child of Emperor Tiberius Caesar and his mother a prostitute. Lucius feared what Valencia would think if she knew. He'd told her very little of his past, thinking she would be ashamed to be seen with a banished son with no future. "I miss her."

He thought if he and Val had met under different circumstances, they would be able to wed. Being a Captain, marriage was not permitted. On top of that, he had made a vow to never sire an heir to his father. He pushed that thought out of his mind. Sadness prickled his thoughts—the woman he loved was so close that he could taste her, yet she was so far away. *What was she thinking? Fooling around with a guy like me with no real family or future?* Lucius thought. She had so much more to lose than he did, which made him feel extremely selfish. It made him pull her tighter against himself and wonder if his mother had been loved in this way once upon a time, before politics drove her away and ended in her execution, resulting in his banishment to the guard. The silver lining was meeting Val.

Val raised on her elbow and pulled the sheets up around her porcelain skin modestly as she splayed her open palm across his chest, right where his heart drummed. Her half-smile, half-

grimace comforted him. He had sworn an oath to
Caesar that so long as he was a member of the
ranks, he would not marry; he would not have an
heir. Common-law marriage was beginning to be
accepted, but a tetrarch's daughter would never be
permitted to engage in such base relationships.
Children of gubernatorial leaders were married off
in political matches, adding to the reputation of
their parents. He knew that, but it still was hard to
accept.

"It's hard, isn't it?" She kissed his
shoulder. "Do you ever wonder who your father
was?"

He had hidden the gruesome details from
her on purpose, and he would continue to do so
until he could find a way to approach the man.
Lucius had always known he was the illegitimate
son of Tiberius Caesar, but his mother had sworn
him to secrecy. And after watching her attempts to
help him find favor in the emperor's eyes, and
being put to death under accusation of an
attempted coup, Lucius was fearful that if he said
anything, his fate would match hers.

"It matters very little who my father is,
Val." He cupped her cheek and brushed his thumb
over her high cheekbone as his fingers tangled in
her curly hair. "The oath of the guard is not
something to be taken lightly. Rebellion against

the order means death. I cannot find favor with Pilate or Caesar. This is my fate." A fate he had chosen and accepted, no matter how much he hated it. He believed it was the only way to prove his name and get the attention of his father.

"Then leave the guard. Leave the guard and marry me." Valencia's words were so innocent, so endearing, Lucius may very well have done as she asked if his conscience would allow him. But doing so would have them both on the streets.

"I can't. You know that."

"Then I will go to my father. He will make the change."

"Val, if you go to your father you will only make things worse. He will prohibit you from seeing me. And if he finds out we've been intimate… taking advantage of each other, it's my head on the block." He chuckled.

Valencia collapsed down onto him again, this time with a frown. He hated to make her feel this way, but they both knew before they began this course what it would mean. Love mattered very little to the state. War, sacrifice, loyalty— those were what mattered. Though Lucius wrestled with himself about what was right, he had sworn to serve the state.

"Then I will pray to Juno. She will grant me a favor. We can be together, Lucas." She giggled hopefully.

How I wish it would be so. He thought silently to themself and he did wish it so, more than anything. Lucius had spent years of his life training in the guard, working his way up the ranks. He had achieved the rank of centurion faster and at a younger age than anyone else in history. Many of his commanders had lauded his cunning and resilience, remarking how he reminded them of the emperor in so many ways. How many times had Lucius wanted to tell them all he was Caesar's son? How many times had he been mistreated and wished to use his lineage to his advantage, but his mother's warning always rang true in his heart?

Be your own man, Luca. Show the world you have the blood of kings in your veins, but do not tell them. No one has to tell a crowd when a lion walks into the room.

He had never been certain of what his mother had meant, but he gained a different sense of understanding with every passing day.

"Juno will grant us a favor, Lucius."

"Juno is a stone carved and positioned in corners of kings' palaces and nothing more." Lucius chuckled and tried not to be cynical, but he'd given up hope that the gods could or would do anything to help him, especially after he watched his mother be put to death. He grew serious. Juno had done nothing for her.

"I'm sorry." Valencia pulled away from him and slid off the bed. He watched as she walked away, finding her dressing gown and pulling it over her head. Part of him wanted to comfort her. He knew she fully believed in the gods. But part of him was so bitter toward the gods she worshipped and the faith she had that he remained lying there, watching her prepare to leave.

"I will come by tomorrow."

And with those parting words, she gathered the rest of her belongings and stepped into the outer room. Regret for not calling her back crept in and soured his night further. If he could be like other men, just dedicate himself to the state and drown his sorrows in sex and wine more often, he may be happier. But a feeling of desire constantly nagged at him. There had to be more to life than this. There has to be more than just power. Life isn't just about money, fame, sex, status, and the constant push to being better than the next person. However, it seems, that could be all anyone has ever strived for. With that last thought, Lucius rolled over and dreamed of Val and him in another life.

Chapter Three

Lucius's eyes bolted open. The pitch black of the night teemed with shouts from the street below, jolting him awake. He threw back the covers and slung his feet to the ground, the cold stone jarring his senses for a moment as he gained his balance and stumbled toward the low window. Flickers of light danced on his ceiling, cast from below. He groaned and cursed under his breath.

"Why can't I just have one night off?"

Staying out of sight, he hovered in the window and watched the disruption unfold below him. More than a hundred men pushed and crammed their way down the narrow path between buildings, holding torches, cursing, yelling accusations and insults that made no sense to him.

They shoved a man ahead of them, his hands bound. The man looked calm despite the angry crowd jostling him and herding him to the house of Pilate, the Roman Governor.

"Seriously?" Lucius grumbled and headed for the pile of clothing on the floor next to his bed where he'd thrown it. He knew the guards standing watch would be upon his doorstep in a matter of moments, so he dressed with haste, donning his breastplate and helmet and strapping on his scabbard. He had only just tied his sandals on when the knock came.

"Captain?" It was Sebastian at the door.

"Coming." Lucius barked.

As soon as he swung the door open, he was greeted with a jumbled barrage of information from Sebastian and another officer named Tumas. Keeping the peace in the city was his job, so getting to the bottom of the chaos quickly was his top priority. They barely took a breath as they spewed out what they knew of the current chaos. Their words jumbled together into unintelligible noise until Lucius held a hand up to stop them.

"One of you at a time!" His men stared at him wide-eyed, so he gestured to Sebastian. "Speak."

"Sir, it's the Jews. They have had a trial of one of their own, and they are headed to Pilate's house."

"In the middle of the night?" Lucius glanced over his shoulder at Sebastian in confusion. "Who holds a trial in the middle of the night?"

"Political leaders who are up to no good and out for personal gain." Tumas' gravelly voice reverberated around the stone walls of the stairwell as they descended to the street.

"Yes." Sebastian opened the door for Lucius. "We believe the man they have in custody is the Jew everyone has been talking about. The one who is reported to have performed miracles and raised the dead. Jesus."

Lucius's ears pricked up to those words, and he picked up his pace to a jog, now chasing down the crowd. "Tumas, send for a disbursement. We will need help controlling the people. Sebastian, come with me." He turned down an alley that would bring them closer to the governor's mansion, a faster way than the Jews were leading Jesus.

"Why, Sebastian?" With each step he took, his confusion grew deeper. "Why would the Jews bring one of their own to the governor? Don't they have their system set up? Why get the crown involved?"

"I don't know, sir." Sebastian's tone had lost all familiarity.

They approached the mansion with enough time to follow Jesus being pushed into the praetorium, the official residence of the Roman governor presiding over Jerusalem. It was then that Lucius noticed a detachment of troops with the only other captain in the city already with the prisoner. One of his comrades-in-arms, Captain

Felix, ordered the troops. They escorted Jesus into the building where Lucius could see a very sleepy Pontius Pilate taking his place in the governor's seat. Lucius took his place in the guard as the troops positioned the man in front of Pilate's seat and stood back.

"Is this true that you're King of the Jews?" He did not look at the prisoner as if he thought the man guilty; instead, his eyes were deep, questioningly intense.

"If you say it is so," Jesus replied solemnly.

At that moment, chaos erupted. The chief priests and elders lost their control and started shouting and running for the prisoner.

"He deserves to die! If he were not a criminal, we would not have handed him over to you!"

"He speaks blasphemy! We have no right to execute anyone. Crucify him!"

"No one dishonors our laws, there is only one way and one law!" they spat at Jesus.

Pilate held his hand up to silence them.

Lucius was shocked by the furious outburst of grown men in leadership positions. *Why did he not defend himself?* he thought. Lucius knew that the high priests and elders cared more about their laws than people. However, something told him this outburst was more about hurt pride rather than just

26

broken law. Besides, he didn't say anything blasphemous. If he had broken their previous law, why not stone him? This prisoner intrigued him. Most men would fight back or at least ask not to be put to death. However, here he was, solemnly silent hearing everything that he was accused of doing.

Pilate took the prisoner aside and moved closer to the guard to avoid another strenuous outburst. Questioning Jesus himself without yelling would be much more clarifying.

"Your people and chief priests handed you over to me. What have you done?" Pilate whispered in frustration.

Jesus looked around at the guard. Seemingly looking for someone to hear him and understand, he said, "My kingdom does not consist of what you see around you. If it did, my servants would fight so that I wouldn't be handed over to the Jews. But I'm not that kind of king. Not the world's kind of king."

"So, are you a king or not?" Pilate replied, bewildered. His reaction mimicked the rest: pure bafflement.

Lucius traded a *"what the hell"* glance at Sebastian. This Jew was insane, but why did the way he spoke and acted intrigue them all? He spoke in a calm but serious voice, so confident but still soft. Jesus did not stutter or hesitate before he spoke. He spoke it as if it was truth and wisdom. Most men's confidence had them loud and arrogant. Was he mad or telling the truth?

How strange, Lucius thought.

Jesus spoke again, looking directly at Pilate in the eye. "Because I am a king, I was born and entered the world so that I could witness to the truth. Everyone who cares for truth, who has any feeling for the truth, recognizes my voice."

Pilate averted his eyes uncomfortable and asked "What is truth?"

Jesus did not reply. He simply looked heartbroken. Pilate stormed out of the room pondering what to do.

Sebastian let out an audible gasp, and Lucius began to understand why the Jewish leaders might want this man gone. He admitted to being king of the heavens, but something about the way he spoke troubled Lucius. He spoke as if he were not mortal, as if he knew more than any soul—a blasphemous claim at best, but hardly worthy of being tried before the Roman government.

"Why are they trying this man in the Roman court?" Lucius asked him again as if he would have the answer, his voice hushed so as not to draw attention to themselves. Sebastian knew less about the Jewish leaders' affairs than he did. The question had no answer, as neither of them had been privy to whatever plan had been put in place, though he wondered why Roman guards had been tasked to accompany the prisoner. Normally, involving soldiers required payment, and by the look of the crowd, it must have been a heavy bribe. Lucius shifted uncomfortably as the shouts from around the front of the praetorium swelled.

"He is a blasphemer!"

"He deserves death!"

The shouts calmed as Pilate addressed them, seeking to release Jesus to them. Lucius could tell the governor wanted nothing to do with the death of this man. The Jews who had paraded the man in shackles across the city now called for his punishment, even for his death. Lucius couldn't understand what the man had done that would warrant death; he wasn't violent, just a little delusional. As Lucius thought that, his heart remembered the inhuman way the man had spoken, unlike any of the men Lucius had met who lusted after power, wealth, and status. The Jew didn't even defend himself, yet he was so certain in his speaking. Lucius had to sort this out before the city ripped itself apart over this man. If Jesus of Nazareth were to be convicted on Pilate's words, it would happen in less than twelve hours, before the sun was vertical.

After a few minutes of trying to reason with the angry mob outside, Pilate returned. He barked orders at the detachment of troops to have Jesus be taken to Herod since he was in town. The man was trouble the governor did not want to deal with.

"Sebastian, come on." Lucius nodded. "We have to get to the bottom of this before they start rioting."

Sebastian pondered aloud. "Why would Thermeris send his guards to arrest an innocent man? He can't be innocent if he's standing before Pilate. No one would trouble the governor at an early hour of the day."

Recalling their conversation last night that Lucias chalked to just gossip, he asked, "Tell me everything you have heard of this Jesus."

"Lucius . . ."

"What word have you heard?"

"I've heard only good, noble, and unbelievable things, but I'd have to see them with my own eyes to believe the claims people are talking about." Sebastian averted his eyes. "Lucius, these people are out for his blood."

"You will accompany me to investigate, and Tumas can lead the guards in controlling the crowds." Lucius glanced at the horizon, the first fingers of the sun barely taking hold in the distant sky. "Now, report to Tumas, and return here at once."

Sebastian looked hesitant at first, like he wanted to object, but nodded and took on a more serious look. "Sir." With no further protest, Sebastian set off.

32

Chapter Four

Lucius stood to watch outside the arena where Herod questioned Jesus, leaning on a pillar. Following more intense questioning at the governor's mansion, and upon finding out the man was a Galilean, Pilate sent Him to Herod. The move seemed to make sense to Lucius, who understood the dynamic involved, and he helped escort them across town. Now, too far to hear Jesus being questioned and busy with crowd control, Lucius decided he would investigate further. Sebastian also gathered intel from a few angry mob members. He kept side-eying Lucius with concern. This whole situation made Lucius uneasy.

"What are you doing?" Valencia's hiss stopped Lucius's heart. He spun on his heel and faced her glare. She wore her hair swept up and knotted on top of her head, a thin veil draped across it and covering her neck and shoulders. The deep blue material accented the green flecks in her eyes that sparkled in the morning's first light.

"Why are you here?" The question must have been the wrong thing to ask because Val's face contorted into an even angrier scowl. Her nostrils flared, and her nose twitched.

"My father is a part of Pilate's council. I am here for support. You, Lucius, are not a lawyer, nor on the council, so you need to be more focused on controlling the crowd rather than interrogating them."

"Val, you shouldn't be here." Though he was slightly irritated with her, he knew she only wanted to take care of him.

"Neither should you. This is Jewish business, and they shouldn't have involved Rome. Also, I don't have a good feeling about this." A worrisome look painted her face overlooking the crowd. "Look how angry the people are with this so-called Jesus." She crossed her arms over her chest then shot him an angry pout.

Lucius sighed knowingly. He too had an uneasy feeling. On top of everything, he had execution duty today, and he wanted to make amends with Val after last night. He could tell she was more concerned about making amends after last night than the city that was about to come apart. This day was getting worse by the minute. The executions were always a difficult duty for him to fulfill, and he always visited Val before. It helped him stomach it. In her eyes, he saw anger laced with disappointment and hurt.

"I promise to make this up to you after my shift. I don't know when I will finish but . . ." *I love you*, he thought silently. "You should go home. It's not safe." He did not know how he would make anything up to her, but she was his world, the only person who cared for him. He snatched her hand and glanced around the street, making sure no one was looking. Everyone had their eyes trained on the trial happening down the front. He held her fingers between his, more affection than should be shown in the street, and pulled her chin up so he could look in her eyes. Hoping she could see the unspoken *I love you* in his eyes. He did love her desperately but would never say it. They couldn't be together; therefore, innocent *I love you's* would only make it harder when she was married off.

"Please come with me," Val begged. "I don't have a good feeling about this."

"I'm on duty, Val," he said sternly. Lucius was a man of this word. "After all, it's my job to uphold truth and justice." He said half-heartedly rolling his eyes trying to lighten the mood. "Go home and be safe." He kissed her cheek and walked forward to take his place amongst the emerging guards and prisoners. He glanced at the commotion down front where Herod's men draped one of his purple robes around the prisoner. It seemed that the tetrarch was mocking the Jew, the so-called King rousing the crowd to taunting jests.

As he walked away, he whispered out of her earshot, "I love you."

He walked with his hand on his sword, matching the demeanor of the other guards as they escorted the prisoner back down the winding streets toward Pilate's home. A stranger slammed into him, causing him to semi-stumble into another man. People shoved and hit at the guard to get to Jesus. A scuffle broke out, and a few guards had to leave the catchment to handle the crowd. Lucius focused on moving the prisoner and was relieved when they returned to Pilate's house. Entering the gate, leaving the crowd behind, he saw Tumas approaching.

"Captain!" Tumas shouted. He came up and stroked alongside Lucius with the rest of the guard that ushered Jesus in behind them. A confident young soldier and had excelled quickly in the ranks, Lucius was confident that Tumas had all the potential to be a captain one day.

"Captain, they're taking the prisoner before Pilate to be questioned again. The Jews refuse Herod's claim of innocence. They are demanding his death, and Pilate will only scourge him."

"What the hell is happening?" Lucius rolled his eyes. He knew he was in for a very long shift.

"This man here hasn't done anything, and now they want him to die because he upset them? Since when do we put people to death because they don't like them?"

"I don't know, sir. Though I have other news on this interesting day. This is confidential information, Captain." Tomas leaned in closer and brought his voice to a whisper. "Pilate was furious after this morning and demanded that Captain Felix and the guards who brought Jesus to be questioned. He wanted to know why they had to involve Rome. As we suspected, a large bribe was part of it. Pilate is trying to keep his hands clean of Jesus, so he'll let the Jews decide who they want to put to death: Barabbas or Jesus." Tumas then averted his eyes nervously. " Felix was discharged. You are now the only captain in the city."

Lucius signed, bowing his head in his hands. He let that fact sink in. This was not good. The city peace was now only his responsibility, and the city was tearing itself apart at the moment. "By the looks of this riot, we will need all troops on duty," Lucius commanded.

"Yes, sir."

Lucius swallowed hard. At least he would have direct access to this prisoner, and perhaps even to Pilate. He could ask the questions he was dying to know. *Had he healed the sick? Raised the dead? And forgive the unforgivable sins? What mere man could forgive sins?* Lucius had never been more curious, intrigued, and frustrated than with this situation. If he could convince Pilate to throw out the case, a possibly innocent man could go free. This bolstered his hope and brought a calmness over him.

"Very good then, Tumas. Find Sebastian. Make sure the guards have the city under control. Keep the peace."

"Sir." Tumas turned to leave, but Lucius called after him.

"Tumas."

"Yes, sir."

"You're a good man. Don't waste your life on the guard. It's unfulfilling and lonely. Find a woman you love, and don't let her go."

The comment drew a smile to Tumas' lips and a nod. "Of course, sir."

Chapter Five

On his way back to Pilate's, Lucius noticed Valencia had not done what he had asked her to do—not entirely. She had gone from him before the crowds got too raucous, but she had not returned to the safety of her residence. She stood along the edge of the crowd, watching on as Jesus was being forced back to Pilate's home. She had her back to him and stood on her tiptoes, craning her neck, her blue gown dusting the earth as she wobbled.

Lucius rushed to her side and grabbed her elbow, turning her toward him. She did not look surprised at all to see him there, almost as if she were expecting him to come. She wrenched her arm away as he shouted over the roar of the crowd.

"Why didn't you go home?"

"I want to see what happens." The veil over her head had fallen, so he reached for it, but she shrugged away.

"I..."

"Lucas, I am as curious as you. You dissuade me from being involved in politics, but there are plenty of women here." She gestured at the crowd, and she was indeed correct, though most of the women remained toward the back of the crowd, and nearly all of them were Jewish.

He gritted his teeth. He only wanted to protect her, and she was insolent. "I asked you to go home. This is not a peaceful riot." These crowds were dangerous, and she was noble and vulnerable.

She reached out and took his hand, smiling at him coyly. "Then come with me. There is such a distraction, surely you will not be missed for hours." Batting her eyes at him, she pulled him a few steps from the crowd.

"Please go home, Valencia."

The use of her full name drew a look of pain, as if he'd slapped her across the cheek rather than the scolding it was. She withdrew her hand and her chin dropped for a moment before she looked back at him with tears in her eyes.

"Are you my father, that you can order me? My husband?"

"I am your commander." The tone he took he only meant to be for her protection, but he could see the hurt in her expression as she blinked hard, the tears still escaping. *I love you. I need you safe.* He thought this in silence, hoping it would be enough to make her go home. The way the day was shaping out wasn't promising to end on a good note. He selfishly needed to have peace of mind that she was safe. That would be the only thing getting him through the day. She backed away from the crowd and turned from him, her head down.

Silently, he cussed to himself as he watched her walk away for the second time. He had to force himself not to follow her, despite his desire to swoop in and make things right with her, but his duty called, and she would be safe away from this rioting mess. He needed answers. He needed to search out the truth, so he turned and pushed his way past the masses, using his authority as a centurion to gravitate toward the front of the crowd. On the way, he bumped into one of the Jewish elders; he could tell by the man's robe, with the fine blue threads sewn onto the garment's wings. Something inside of him urged him to stop and speak to the man.

"Excuse me," Lucius said, resting his hand on the hilt of his sword as he often did to display his authority. The man faced him, and Lucius sensed the man was angry.

"What?"

"I can't help but wonder why you Jews would bring your criminal to the governor. What has he done that is so bad that he must be tried before Pilate?" Lucius awaited an answer eagerly.

"We have laws, and he has broken our laws. And our laws state that this man must die for what he has done. That is all you need to know."

Lucius pondered his statement for a moment and went to walk away, but something stirred him to continue questioning. "But, sir, if you have laws, then certainly you could enact your own punishments."

"It is not lawful for us to carry out such a sentence as he deserves on our holiest days. Surely you understand that—or do you anger Mars and Jupiter purposefully?"

The man's response had Lucius biting his tongue. He knew better than to engage in a religious debate with a scholar, and he had no desire to do so, so he pressed on, questioning as many men as he could as he continued toward the praetorium. Each time he addressed one of the Jewish leaders, he was given the same answer; only once did anyone show the slightest hint that something was awry. Even then, the man who had shown remorse had only parroted the words spewed out by the other leaders: Jesus was guilty because he claimed to be the son of God, guilty of treason, guilty of blasphemy.

Lucius found his way inside the praetorium and strolled up to a few other guards watching. He thought to ask their opinions, but the sight unfolding before him demanded his attention. At once, he stopped and listened to what Pilate said. The crowd jeered him on, but Pilate remained calm.

"I find no fault in him," Pilate announced.

Lucius' heart soared. The governor would acquit the man and he would go free, and this nonsense would be ended. He watched Pilate with his entourage exit toward the porch and listened as he addressed the people. He could barely hear the words said as his thoughts spun, but he thought he heard Pilate tell the angry mob he would have the man scourged and released.

At that mention, he was saddened again as he looked to the man who stood bound before him. He studied Jesus of Nazareth for a moment. He looked no different than any other Jewish man: brown hair, brown eyes, olive skin. He was nothing special to look at, not like Roman men who paraded their physique. The Jew was plain, but he looked fit despite being just a teacher, as if he did manual labor. And when his eye turned toward Lucius, he felt a warmth surge through him, a strange fullness and peace.

Jesus of Nazareth did not appear to be a criminal. There was a kindness in his gaze, a gentleness like that of a father, despite the crowd hurling insults at him demanding his death. Lucius thought of what the Jewish elders had said of him and decided they must be mistaken. How could this man standing in front of him be guilty of something worthy of death? He had not killed anyone, nor had he harmed a woman. He had not even stolen, which was a much lesser crime. All Lucius had heard about the man was how he had done countless miracles. Things Lucias would have liked to see to believe, yet here he was being tried for treason and certain elders of them were calling for his death.

"Take him out. You there," Pilate stated, "captain, this man is to be scourged and returned to me."

Lucius locked eyes with the governor. "Yes, sir."

Pilate was only doing this in hopes of appeasing the crowd. A lump formed in his throat as he approached the Jew, the warmth and peace within him growing stronger by the minute. He approached Jesus and took him by the elbow. The man went willingly, like a lamb to the slaughter, without a word. Lucius wanted to ask him why they hated him so, but a great sadness overtook him, and he could find no words. He could only escort the prisoner to the scourging post.

Chapter Six

As Lucius and his prisoner entered the scourging area, guards dragged a different man away, a thief who would be executed later on. The man's face was bruised, bloodied, his ear partially torn off. *That* man was a criminal; *that* man deserved what was coming to him. Lucius's eyes turned toward the Jew again, somber, but strangely not frightened. He looked determined in a way. Like he was on a mission. This intrigued Lucius and added more mystery to this ever-evolving puzzle. This man had done nothing worthy of death so far as he could tell, and he was grateful that Pilate had ordered him to be scourged and released. He hoped it would be enough for the Jewish religious leaders, the beating and warning.

He scanned the room, noticing the angry looks on several guards' faces. They appeared to be made for moments like this. Lucius was a hard captain known for being cunning, though he did not find enjoyment in beating men to the very inch of their life.

"Here." One of Thermeris' men approached with a leather cord in hand. He yanked on Jesus' bound wrists and caused him to fall to the ground, then he dragged him to the pillar. The younger guard seemed to enjoy dishing out the punishment, and Lucius could not understand what type of a person it took to severely harm another defenceless person. Lucius never shied away from a fight or violence. He was Caesar's son, after all. He excelled faster than anyone in the ranks. However, his soft spot was innocence. His mother had been innocent. He found it distasteful and unfair to whip a tied-up man and often wondered if his mother had been scourged like this.

He took in the arena. In here, the coppery stench of blood permeated the air. Old blood stained the floor and walls. A few rows of benches lined the walls, the pillar in the center their focus. He noticed several men seated as if ready to observe, and then he recognized Cicero Anatolia Amata, Valencia's father, seated next to his commander.

Lucius's feet felt like stone blocks. He cussed to himself as he slowly made his way past the prisoner bound to the pillar. *Why am I here? Just because you're on the council doesn't mean you have to watch this. Why do men love blood and violence?*

"Let's get this started. We haven't got all day." Cicero stood and clapped his hands a few times before sitting back down, seemingly excited to watch this Jew get beaten to a pulp. Lucius shuddered slightly, thinking of his mother, as two guards tore the Jew's garments down the back, exposing his skin. The man looked him in the eye, and he swore he saw compassion there for a moment.

"Here." The younger guard who had bound the prisoner shoved a tool in Lucius' hand, a long rod with several leather straps affixed to it. On the ends of the leather strands were pieces of sharp metal.

The cat's tail whip, Lucius thought. They used this for and especially bloody bleatings, nearly bringing prisoners to the brink of death normally.

Laughter rose from the guards as Lucius watched them laugh and poke fun at Jesus. This could be his chance to impress Val's father, even his commander. He could perhaps earn favor and move up in rank—a long shot to be able to provide a way for him and Valencia to be married. As if thinking of her could make her appear, there she was, standing in the doorway of the scourging area, watching him.

His eyes met hers for a long moment, even as the whips of the other guards began to tear into the Jew's skin. The thorn and bramble switches were nothing compared to the weapon Lucius held in his own hands. Each crack of a whip made him want to look at what was happening, but the pity in his beloved's eyes kept him fixed there.

"Finish this one," one of the guards shouted urging him on with glee in his voice.

"Yes, a good show please!" Val's father bellowed.

Lucius raised his hand back to strike, but he could not will himself to do it. Jesus was innocent, just like his mother. The urge to cry out and free the man was strong, but not enough to make him stop. Still, it was enough to make him pause and glance back at Val. She looked at her father, and Lucius felt his heart wrench. He had to make a choice: please the leadership and perhaps someday be able to be with Valencia openly, or do what he knew was right. His heart tore down the middle as he swung the weapon forward.

The metal pierced the Jew's side and the crowd erupted in cheers. Lucius tried to draw back to swing again, but the metal was stuck in the man's skin.

"Pull harder!" the guards shouted.

Lucius drew back hard, yanking the whips back. He pulled so hard, he nearly lost his balance. The commander had a malicious grin on his face, and though Lucius found it disturbing, he swung again, connecting this time with Jesus' shoulder. One of the straps wrapped around his head and sunk into his face, which was already black and blue from the beating the other guards had given him. The jeers and taunts only grew more raucous. The guards laughed and pointed, and one of them kicked Jesus' side. He collapsed to the ground, curling into a ball. Blood oozed from every wound on his back.

The way Jesus responded troubled him. King of the Jews? Son of God? If he had claimed to be the son of Zeus, would they have acted this way? If he was the Son of God, why wasn't God coming to save him now? As Jesus absorbed the whipping, not a sound escaped his lips. *Who was this man...?* Lucius practically screamed in his thoughts.

Another taller guard took the weapon from Lucius' hands and jerked it upward, tearing a chunk of flesh from Jesus' face. Bits of skin and tissue clung to the metal barbs, and the man pulled them off before thrusting the weapon back into Lucius' hands.

He looked down at the bloodied man, almost unrecognizable. He could feel Valencia's eyes on his back as he swung the weapon, again and again, each strike tearing a bit more of his heart into pieces. He was the judge in this place, delivering punishing blows onto the back of his mother. And when Jesus looked up into his eyes, blood streaming from gashes all over his face. When Lucius saw the love still there, he broke. He could not swing another time.

"We're done." He had never done this, but enough was enough. No one would be able to differentiate this man from a beast in the field. He looked toward his commander, squaring his shoulders, but knowing it wouldn't be right to go on. Instead of disdain, he saw pride in the commander's eyes. His heart sank just a little further knowing this was the way the world was, but he was thankful the scourging was over, and he could wash his hands of this mess.

Lucius dropped the weapon at his feet and turned, catching Valencia's eyes. Her sorrowful expression pained his heart, so he fixed his eyes on Jesus. He wanted to be away from this place and rush to her side, but he remained where he was, dutifully carrying out his orders.

The guards brought Jesus to his feet and cut the bindings from his wrist, and Lucius led him by his elbow past Val and out the door, toward the praetorium where Pilate would inspect the effects of the scourging, and then his job would be over. The man was barely able to stand and leaned heavily on Lucius.

Jesus would go free now. That thought made Lucius smile. Strange, he never let himself get attached to prisoners, mainly because they were scum and criminals. But Jesus seemed kind and was innocent. Maybe one day he would find the man and ask him what the big deal was, but he probably wouldn't want to talk to the man in charge of his flogging. Lucius sighed at that thought. To be disliked wasn't exactly a new thing for his line of work especially in Jerusalem.

Chapter Seven

Stumbling along the corridor, his muscles feeling the exhaustion of the emotion of the day and the exertion from the beating, Lucius led the man to the center of the praetorium. Only then did he realize his hands were stained with blood. He looked down on his clothing; it, too, had a smattering of the dark red liquid across it. He wiped at his breastplate, but the blood had already dried there. Jesus looked up at him and weakly smiled, and Lucius was confused. He had just beaten this man bloody, and yet he smiled as if to thank him.

Outside, he could still hear the crowd carrying on; the cacophony of shouts and angry voices made his head hurt. He slunk back against a wall, scrubbing his palms over his pants, hoping to wipe some of the blood away, but it was no use. As he stood waiting for Pilate to return, Sebastian and Tumas shuffled in, at first looking around the room and then zeroing in on him and heading his way. Both had wide eyes as they gazed upon Jesus of Nazareth.

"What is the report?" Lucius asked them both when they stood before him.

Sebastian spoke first. He seemed exhausted, his normal professional demeanor lost to the chaos of the day. "Lucius, he is an innocent man. The worst claim we could come up with was that he turned over tables in the temple and disrupted their worship. He's done nothing but heal the sick and teach people to follow their religion."

"Yeah. He hasn't done anything punishable by the Roman courts." Tumas folded his arms over his chest as if he were confident, but his eyes betrayed him, questioning Lucius.

The words settled in Lucius' heart, verifying what he had felt all along. His men had engaged in the city and discovered the accusations against Jesus to be false. Lucius was certain the scourging was given only because Pilate feared the Jews would protest if he did nothing. With only one current centuria in Jerusalem, over two months before he could call additional guards, Lucius decided Pilate had done the political thing, but the correct thing. If they had to maintain the peace of the city, this was the way to do it.

A commotion across the room drew everyone's attention. Lucius watched Pilate enter from the porch and move closer to Jesus. A bit of discourse happened, but he could not hear what was said. Then a few guards came forward, carrying what looked like a few thorny vines which they had twisted into a ring. Pilate gestured to Jesus, and the men placed the ring on his head as if it were a crown. Blood trickled out of the wounds it created, matting his hair and dripping down his already bloodied back.

Pilate said with a little more volume that made the whole room still instantly, "Don't you know that I have the authority to pardon you, and the authority to crucify you?"

Jesus answered confident and calmly, "You haven't a shred of authority over me except what has been given you from Heaven. The one who betrayed me to you has committed a far greater fault."

The words silenced the governor who had a look of indignation on his face. Taking Jesus by the arms, the guards pushed him toward the porch. Lucius followed, fully expecting Pilate to admonish the crowd for their behavior, let Jesus go, and disperse the people. He crept up behind the pavement where Pilate sat down in his judgment seat. Pilate spoke to the people as if he were prepared to release Jesus, but the crowd grew angrier.

"Behold your King!" Pilate shouted, but the men in the crowd began a chant.

"Crucify him!" they screamed, louder and louder until Lucius was sure the very pillars of the praetorium would collapse.

One of the Jewish elders nearest to Pilate shouted, "We have a law, and according to our law, he ought to die because he made himself the son of God."

Pilate looked afraid. His eyes shifted to his guard, then to his wife, who glared at him. "Don't get mixed up in judging this nobleman," she said. "I've just been through a long and troubled night because of a dream about him."

Finally, Pilate stood. Lucius's heart was in his throat. Jesus had had his punishment. It was time to let him go. He was innocent of all charges.

"Do you want me to release this man or Barabbas?"

"Barabbas!" The crowd screamed.

Like a blow to the gut, the air was sucked from Lucius's body. The custom of pardoning one prisoner at the governor's discretion was expected. It didn't always happen, but it was the right of the governor to do so. The mere idea that Pilate could pardon a thief in exchange for silencing the Jews troubled him. He couldn't help but think he had spent his whole life chasing the approval of his father, and in doing so, he had also sought the approval of men like Pilate, who could put an innocent man to death. It didn't just *feel* wrong; he knew it *was* wrong. The world that he had trusted to be just and true was no more just than the dignity of the man in charge.

Some men nearby passed around a wineskin, so Lucius, not thinking, grabbed the skin and tipped it to his mouth, guzzling the warm tart liquid. Nothing would relieve him of the duty he did not want. Lost in thought about what to do next, he prayed to his gods, to Jesus' God, to any god that would hear him for this shift to be over already. He stood watching as several of the guards under his watch ushered Jesus away to prepare him for crucifixion, and from the corner of his eye saw Sebastian approaching from.

"Are we going to stand by and let this happen, Lucas?" His friend was wide-eyed with shock.

Lucius nodded and spat bile from his mouth. He did not look up at Sebastian. He felt weak, like a coward who could not control his emotions, but at the same time, he felt indignant. To murder, an innocent man was vile, worthy of death, but then, perhaps he *was* worthy of death. "There is nothing we can do. It must be God's will that Jesus must die." He was too weak to even speak on behalf of his mother. It was all replaying itself again as if Bacchus were laughing in his face, mocking him for turning to wine to hide his frailties.

"Very good, sir," Sebastian said disappointed, and looked to the ground.

He hardened his heart and squared his shoulders before turning and striding away. Though he still wrestled with how to feel, he knew that the only hope he had of proving his worthiness of Valencia's love was to perform his duties, hope her father would have favor on them, appeal to Caesar, and allow a civil union. His mother was gone; he had no siblings. He had no real father that cared for him—not even hope, not after seeing what the state had deemed as justice. Val was his life now, and he would do what it took to make sure *she*, not this life of injustice, was his future. He would finally face his father and hopefully have a fulfilling life.

Chapter Eight

After regaining his composure, Lucius started toward the front of the house. He rounded the corner and bumped into Valencia. She carried a wineskin in her hand and a look of compassion on her face. He couldn't bear to look at her, but he forced himself to. Her normally brilliant eyes were dull with emotion he couldn't read, though it could have been a disappointment.

"Drink." She thrust the skin into his hands.

Wine was the last thing on his mind at the moment. He had no thirst, no hunger. His stomach still turned, acid stinging the back of his throat. Deciding the wine might settle his stomach and numb his emotions, he took and drank deeply, then corked the skin and handed it back.

"Thank you."

"Lucius," Val whispered. Her eyes searched with care, consideration, and disappointment.

He wanted to take her into his arms and hold her, feel her nestled against his chest as they did in bed so many times, hoping she could help calm his inner demons. Regret, shame, fear, heaviness, darkness. But here in public, even holding hands was forbidden. He settled for looking into her eyes and searching them for the comfort he needed as the wine slowly permeated his senses, relaxing him, numbing his thoughts.

"Val…" He started to speak but had no words. Did he ask about her father, why he watched and enjoyed it? Did he confess how difficult it was to strike that man, even though he was supposed to be this hard captain? Tell her how unjust and evil the government was, only out for power and favor of the people? Should he open the floodgates of all the emotions and thoughts that raged in his head? Tell her who his father was and how his mother was executed? How he stood by and watched and he was about to stand by and watch Jesus die? How weak and exhausted he felt? Tell her the real reason they could not be wed? She smiled sadly, appearing to understand all the words he could not say.

"I know you thought this was wrong, the entire thing. I don't blame you for doing your duty."

Lucius felt heavy. Not even news from Caesar himself could undo the burden weighing him down. Not now that he knew how he had sold his life to serve and uphold the corrupt powers who ruled over them all.

"This is a political move. My father thinks it is all a move to keep the Jews happy with the leadership so they will play nice. Everyone knows this man is innocent, but if they had released him, my father fears there would have been an uprising."

Anger roiled his insides, recalling the way they watched as he and the other soldiers beat Jesus bloody. He grabbed the wineskin and uncorked it, bringing it to his lips and drinking deeply again. When he had drunk his fill, he shoved it into her hands a little more firmly than he should have. Lucius tried not to let the caged beast out of his chest, but it stirred, ready to lash out at the injustice.

"So they feared an uprising? The man will be put to death to keep the peace?" He took a few steps away and then back, anxiously trying to control his temper. Valencia was not to blame and didn't deserve his outburst. "The Jews can't deal with their prisoner because of the Passover, but they could cause an uprising on the Passover? Does Pilate even know Jewish customs?"

Valencia looked shocked at his outburst, her eyes wide as she snatched his wrist and pulled him behind an acacia (uh-kay-shuh) bush growing along the wall. This was the most he had let his inner thoughts rattle on like this to anyone. Lucius normally kept his burdens and troubles to himself, but it had been a long day.

"Listen to yourself, Lucas. And quiet down. Someone will hear you. You are speaking of the governor." She released his wrist, but her face did not soften. "Do you want to be executed next to them?"

Lucius swallowed his anger but clenched his fists at his sides. It was wrong. It was all wrong and they knew it, but they played a political game with a man's life. He didn't want to be a part of it. Fuming, he turned to go when Val spoke.

"I've been looking into things, you know." Val's eyes were on the ground processing her thoughts as she spoke. "So we could get married."

The words froze Lucius in his steps. He took a deep breath and turned back. Val looked hopeful as she set the wineskin down and offered her hand to him. He glanced around, and seeing no one, he took her hand softly. He knew this was not going to be a pleasant conversation, and he would rather not break her heart now.

"You've been inquiring about me. You shouldn't have done that, Val." He spoke firmly with soft eyes.

"I wanted to see if there were a way we could marry, despite the laws forbidding soldiers to marry." She stared off into the horizon. Her thoughts scattered. "My search turned up something interesting, as you may have guessed.

Why didn't you tell me your father was the emperor?"

"That man is not a father to me, Val."

The confusion came across her beautiful face. *Now is the time to confess, Lucius,* he thought to himself. He sighed.

"I'm a bastard, Val. My mother was executed, and I was sentenced to a life of service to the guard." Saying this out loud for the first time, his voice cracked. He had been running from this all his life, and now admitting it to Val, his beloved, was too much. "I have no favor in Caesar's eyes, and it was a mercy I wasn't executed with my mother. Caesar keeps reports on me and knows of my duties as captain. He has forbidden me to marry or sire an heir."

Pain and heartbreak painted Val's face as angry tears streamed down her face. "What are you talking about?" Her eye darted towards the ground, processing her next thought. "All we have to do is convince him to allow you to marry me. He is the emperor and can overrule the law. Even his own words can be revoked." She spoke exasperatedly.

"Val. I can never marry you. This is my fate." His heart torn in half, he acknowledged the truth from which he'd been running. This was his life: serving power-hungry men, no joy, no love. The gods he hated had decided this was his life.

"Lucas… I love you." Valencia's eyes filled with tears. She reached for him.

Lucius stepped back. He felt the tears brimming over and pushed them back. This needed to be a clean break for her sake. He took a last look at her beautiful face, puffy from crying. *Still the most beautiful girl,* he thought. He turned and walked back to the praetorium.

"I love you, too, Val," Lucius whispered under his breath.

Chapter Nine

The heat of the morning beat down on Lucius's back as he pushed the crowds from the path. Forced to walk alongside Jesus as he hefted the massive wooden beam, he watched as the man fell several times. Each time he fell, Lucius would help him stand and lift the beam back to his shoulder. The crowds taunted and mocked Jesus, and Lucius tried to ignore them unless they got in the way.

Two other guards walked along with him, beside the prisoners they guarded. Twice, someone stepped from the crowd to plead for their lives, but not one person came forward to plead for the life of Jesus. Lucius studied him as they wound through the city, toward Golgotha, where he would be crucified. His face was swollen; Lucius didn't know how he could even see. Blood still oozed from the raw skin of his back and face, his hair matted with dirt and dried blood beneath the makeshift crown. Lucius wanted to tear it from his head and apologize for his mistreatment, but the icy stares from his comrades kept him focused on one thing: finishing his task so he could go home.

As they turned the last corner and started of the city, Jesus fell again, this time the heavy beam falling across his back and pinning him to the ground. Lucius rushed to his side and took hold of the beam, lifting it. Another man took hold along the other side, and together, they laid the beam on the ground.

Lucius nodded to the man in thanks, wiping the back of his arm across his sweaty forehead. The man nodded and stepped back into the crowd as Lucius knelt to check on Jesus. He was panting, dirt now pressed into the cuts and gashes on his face. His lips were chapped and cracking, spit dripping out of the corner of his mouth. He couldn't go on like this; Lucius knew it. He would never make it to the top of the hill.

He glanced at the two men still struggling ahead of where they would drag their beams up the incline, the guards following them, driving them on with whips. Then he looked back down at Jesus. He couldn't very well carry the beam for him and still make sure someone in the crowd didn't abscond with him. He tried to pick Jesus up, but each time, the man stumbled and nearly fell. Lucius turned to the crowd, spying on the man who had helped him with the beam.

"You," he shouted over the deafening roar of the masses. The man pointed toward his chest and looked around, then stepped forward. Lucius motioned for him to come near. "You carry his cross."

With a look of intimidation, the man bent, hoisted the beam to his shoulder, and started forward. Lucius then lifted Jesus to his feet again, this time draping the man's arm over his shoulders and holding him up as they started forward again. His legs shook with the added weight and the mild effects of the wine. Lucius felt the ribs on the left side of Jesus' body, the skin and muscle having been torn away.

At the top of the hill, Lucius was given a reprieve, ordered to stand down and keep the crowd back as the other guards commenced the crucifixions. He couldn't watch; the screams alone were bad enough. Each *thwack* of the mallet on the nails drew gasps from the crowd and shouts of pain from those being nailed to their crosses. He didn't see when they raised the crosses, dropping the heavy beams down into the holes that would keep them erect.

After several long moments, the crowd began to grow quiet. Their angry shouts turned to soft talking, then faded to murmurs and whispers. Lucius turned and gazed up at Jesus, the man who had done nothing wrong. Above his head they'd nailed a sign that read *King of the Jews*—his only crime, saying he was God's child. Lucius didn't know about the Jewish God; he knew only of those gods who had failed him, Jupiter, Bacchus, Mars, the rest. They were silent, uncaring. They'd watched his mother be executed and did not defend her. He wondered why this man's God was watching him die without aiding him. He wondered if the God of the Jews was like the rest—sleeping or dead.

Jesus rolled his head back toward the sky, and raising on his legs so he could take a breath, he spoke. His voice was raspy, but he choked out the words. "Father, forgive them; they don't know what they're doing."

Lucius felt tears sting his eyes at the heart of this man. That he should pray to his God for the forgiveness of those who were harming him, despite his innocence. He stood there for hours, staring at Jesus. When his legs grew tired, he knelt, but his eyes stayed fixed on the man. There was a rustle of activity farther down the hill, and a guard ran up with a pail and a sponge on a stick. They sopped the sponge in the bucket and raised the stick to Jesus' mouth, the dark liquid dripping down his body across his wounds. He turned away bitterly, and they left him alone.

The sun still beating down on the crowds, some men began to disperse, though many stayed and watched on. Sweat drenched Lucius' clothing, but he kept his armor on. He looked down at his hands, still stained with Jesus' blood from the scourging, and stared at them, feeling numb. Guilt hung over his heart, even after hearing Jesus pray for his forgiveness. At that moment, he thought it should be him on that cross. He should be the one dying, not because he wished for death, but because he was guilty of things that were deserving of death. He thought of all the unspeakable things he had done for the guard and Rome. He was no different than his father or Pilate. Always wanting more power, money, and respect. The world was a sinful place.

He heard talking coming from the crowds again and looked up at Jesus. He was painstakingly raising himself again to breathe. Each time he did it appeared to take a much greater effort. Lucius could hear his labored breathing, wheezing and gasping for air. He was heartbreaking to watch. "Father, I place my life in your hands!" Jesus collapsed back down, his body hanging by the nails that pierced his hands. Then once more, he pushed, struggling to hoist himself up again. Women in the crowd sobbed and wailed. Men murmured angry slurs and spoke in harsh tones. "It is finished."

The last words were so quiet, Lucius could barely hear them. What did that mean? What he had finished? He stood and took one step forward when the Earth began to rumble. It started low and rose to a clamor. A deafening crack of thunder filled the sky as black clouds descended blocking out the sun. Screams of hysteria and fear broke out, and men and women began fleeing. The ground started to shake and losing his balance, Lucius stumbled forward into another guard. Together the two clung to each other as the world around them erupted into chaos. Large boulders tumbled from the hill, rolling down onto the people. The crosses rattled in their holes, waving around in the air wildly. It was black as midnight, though Lucius knew it was nearly the ninth hour. There had been no clouds in the sky only moments ago. He stood with eyes wide open yet seeing nothing. Minutes passed and finally, the shaking stopped.

Lucius let go of the guard, who trembled in fear. He, too, was terrified. Light began to pierce through the dark clouds and shone directly on Jesus. Lucius and a few of the guards stood dumbfounded, staring at Jesus. The clouds rolled out. The strange phenomena left them shellshocked. An earthquake, a black sky, and the man's final words, *It is finished.* Lucius was overcome by a sensation he'd never felt before. The warmth of the man's gaze while standing in the praetorium had not filled his heart like this.

His God had spoken, not with words, not with messengers and teachers. His God had shaken the earth, blackened the sky; He had thundered from Heaven.

Lucius marveled at it all, whispering to himself and the other guards. "Surely this man was the Son of God."

With the crowds now gone, his job had been fulfilled. Lucius stumbled away from the other guards, baffled and in awe.

Chapter Ten

The streets were empty after the earthquake.
Lucius pushed his way through some debris and
began making his way home down the narrow
streets lined with stone buildings. Men who passed
by or walked alongside him talked about the
strange happenings, but Lucius, still trying to make
sense of what had happened, was too lost in
thought to engage in conversation. He'd gone from
utterly distraught to mesmerized and entranced.
His head spun.

Several people walked in the same
direction as him, but the crowd began to disperse
quickly. He took his helmet off and carried it, his
hair damp with sweat from the heat. Valencia
entered his thoughts. He wondered what she would
say about the day's events, if she would believe his
witness. Of course, she would have to; there were
hundreds of witnesses to what happened, and she
had to have felt the earthquake. He pushed her out
of his head. He could not be weak, and he had to
let her go.

So many years ago, Lucius had given up all
faith in any god. He'd prayed to Bacchus that the
wine would take away his sorrow. He'd prayed to
Juno to protect his mother. He'd prayed too many

times to too many deities only to have those prayers fall on deaf or non-existent ears. A question began to stir in his heart about the God of Jesus, the God of the Jews. Would this God answer prayers? But how could he become a Jew when he was born Roman? Was it possible for a Roman to become a Jew, and did he even want to be a Jew knowing how religious, heartless and pious their Jewish leaders were? Could a non-Jew even believe in their God?

Lost in thought, he rounded the corner of a wall and rammed into someone running the opposite direction. He lost his balance and slammed into the corner of a building, nearly toppling to his knees. His helmet skittered across the cobble stones, spinning. Lucius watched the man whom he had run into dash away without stopping to see if he was alright.

"Stop! Thief." Another man shouted and ran past, chasing the first man. Lucius sighed and scrambled to put his helmet back on, running after the two. His first two steps were unsteady, his legs tired from the exhausting day, but soon he found his footing.

I'm supposed to be going home, he thought as he raced down the street, steadying his scabbard so it wouldn't bang against his leg. The men turned down an alleyway that led them all closer to the barracks and prisons. People on the street darted out of the way of the pursuit, and Lucius joined in the shouting, urging the criminal to stop fleeing. Seeing the man turn down another street a few houses ahead, Lucius cut away from the path and dodged between two buildings. He moved up a set of stairs across a landing, before working his way across a courtyard, weaving between sheets hung on lines to dry, hoping he could cut off the chase.

He scrambled over a wall, and just as he suspected, the thief darted around the corner. Lucius leapt from the high wall, dropping to the ground just in front of the man, causing a collision. The man rammed into Lucius and tripped. Both of them fell in a heap. The man who had been pursuing the thief caught up to them and stopped, leaning forward with his hands on his knees, catching his breath.

"Sir, this man stole from me!" The accuser bent down and snatched a leather pouch from the hands of the dazed thief. Lucius sat up and rolled the thief over, immediately recognizing the man.

"Barabbas?"

Barabbas rubbed his head and groaned. "You owed me twenty coppers, old man."

"I owe you nothing, you dog." The man kicked Barabbas and opened his pouch. "It's all here, sir. All my money is still here."

Lucius got to his knees and then stood, staring down at Barabbas who started laughing. The old man walked away, leaving Lucius to decide what to do.

"You were just pardoned by the governor himself not hours ago, and you're already back to thieving?" The blood in his veins began to boil. "You realize an innocent man was murdered, and you were let go?"

Barabbas sat up laughing harder. His shoulders shook and his belly jiggled. "I guess I'm a lucky man, then, aren't I?"

"You are coming with me. I'm taking you back to the prisons."

Barabbas bolted to his feet as if to flee, but Lucius was faster, drawing his sword and pointing it at the man's chest.

"Try it."

Barabbas held both hands up in surrender as Sebastian appeared around the corner and came closer to help Lucius. He carried his whip in hand, probably called upon in the ruckus before Lucius joined the chase.

"I did nothing wrong. He has his coins back."

"You? *You* did nothing wrong? You are a liar and a criminal." With Sebastian there to aid him, Lucius sheathed his sword and moved close enough to smell the stench of alcohol on the man's breath. Images of Jesus' marred body hanging on the cross flashed through his mind and the rage boiled over into his fists.

Lucius swung once, his fist connecting to Barabbas' jaw, then again, pounding him on the cheek. Barabbas stumbled back as Lucius' assault continued, blow after blow until the thief fell down, but Lucius didn't stop. His rage had to come out. He straddled Barabbas on the ground and continued to punch him over and over until he felt hands grabbing him beneath his armpits.

Sebastian pulled Lucius off the man, shouting at him to stop, but Lucius didn't want to stop. He wanted justice. He wanted the man who should have died to feel the punishment he'd given Jesus. The man who walked the streets free, who took that liberty and used it to continue stealing. The man who gave no thanks for his freedom.

Barabbas lay weakly chuckling and blood running down his temples as Sebastian shoved Lucius away. He had an angry expression on his face, and had the man been anything other than his friend, Lucius would have had him arrested as well, being a lower rank yet imposing his will over him.

"Enough!" Sebastian planted a foot firmly on Barabbas' chest. "Enough, Lucas. Go home! You're out of control."

The day had been overwhelming, and Lucius had finally snapped. His chest heaving, he shook the pain from his fists and backed away, watching as Sebastian took his whip and bound Barabbas' hands. The thief was still laughing as Sebastian led him away, glancing back a few times with mirth in his expression. Lucius wanted to wipe the smirk off his face.

He heard whispers around him as he turned toward home. Men stood at their gates, women with their washing, speaking in hushed tones about the incident. What on earth could have hardened a man so much that he would be freed from a death sentence only to commit another crime hours later? He rubbed his forehead and sulked as he walked home.

Chapter Eleven

Rounding the corner home, Lucius froze at the sight of a familiar figure in his doorway. Valencia stood like a pillar of hope for a wayward ship that had been lost adrift at sea for months. She held Lucius's robe, a look of love mixed with disappointment and sadness on her face. Lucius was honored that even after his cold, seemingly heartless goodbye, she was here to care for him. She was showing him that she loved him. This act meant she didn't care they could never marry; she loved him more than the life she was entitled to. Lucius had never experienced selfless love like this, except for when he heard Jesus asking for forgiveness of his abusers. Exhausted and overwhelmed, he looked down the barracks' corridor, and seeing that they were alone, he took her into his arms and squeezed her, crushing her auburn curls to his nose so he could breathe in her scent. She welcomed him, embracing him in return.

His helmet clattered to the stone floor behind her, but he didn't care. He never wanted to put that helmet on again. He wanted to steal away with the woman he loved and never return, build a life somewhere outside the reach of Roman authority. His heart couldn't take it anymore.

"I'm here," she said, holding him tightly. He pulled away and unstrapped his breastplate, pulling it over his head and tossing it to the floor beside his helmet. Then he cupped both of her cheeks in his soiled hands and drew her in for a kiss. She tensed at first but then relaxed in his embrace as he deepened the kiss, drinking her in. When he pulled away, her eyes were full of confusion.

He gazed at her with longing but knew it was neither the time nor the place, so he quickly stepped back. "I'm sorry... I just—"

"No, don't be sorry. Today was a difficult day." She stepped forward and draped the robe around his shoulders then took one of his hands and examined it. "You're filthy. You need to go to the baths."

"I do." He shied away, feeling the stain of guilt more as he was reminded of the blood still caked on his hands. "He was innocent, you know?"

"How can you be certain?"

"Sebastian, Tumas, and I asked as many people as we could. It's like your father said, a political move at best." A sudden urge to know the truth sprang up inside his gut like a wildfire. "I just need to know why Val. I just have a feeling this is something more than an execution. I am going to Pilate now. If the answers he gives me do not suffice, I will find answers on my own."

"Oh, Lucas, do you think that's a good idea? You could be reprimanded and sent back to Rome like Thermeris."

"You know about that?"

"My father." She said, rolling her eyes to try and lighten the mood.

"I don't know how I'm feeling, Val. I just sense there was so much more to this Jesus than I saw. The earthquake and clouds . . . it was supernatural." Lucius stood up and shook his head. He had never been this open before with his vulnerability.

"I know, I heard the reports of the light on Jesus, too."

"It was the most baffling event I've ever seen. It made me start to think, maybe there is a God."

"It's got me questioning everything as well. So let's go get those answers, Lucius." She smiled adoringly at him.

Lucius took her hand, and leaving his breastplate and helmet, he pulled her back into the street. They hurried toward the governor's mansion, sunlight slowly fading away. He forced his body to move faster, though it ached for rest. His calves burned as they climbed the small hill, pausing for a moment before opening the gate that led into Pilate's courtyard. Hearing voices on the other side of the gate, Lucius drew a finger to his lips and told Val to remain quiet.

"Sir, if I may."

Lucius immediately recognized the voice without seeing the face. He'd met Joseph of Arimathea on more than one occasion. The man acted as a liaison between the Jews and the government, and multiple times, he had briefed the Roman guard on Jewish festivals and feasts.

"Go on," Pilate responded.

"Sir, if you would permit me, I will take the body and put it in my tomb. It is customary to have the body prepared a certain way for burial in our tradition. The guards can help me roll the stone in place."

Lucius's heart was warmed by the man's gesture.

"Do as you will."

Joseph excused himself, shuffling out the gate and down the street, and Lucius and Val tucked in behind a bush to hide. After a few minutes passed and Lucius regained some sense of confidence, he reached to open the gate and heard another voice, this one angry. It sounded as if their conversation had been cut off earlier, so they were finishing a heated discussion.

"What I'm saying is, he told his disciples that he would rise again. We need guards posted there to make sure they do not steal the body and try to incite a further following."

The voice was arrogant, rude, and coarse. Lucius listened carefully as Pilate replied.

"You have your guards sent now. Leave me alone."

"Sir!" a guard called. "You are needed." Lucius pulled Val back behind a bush as the man slammed the gate open and walked away. All he saw of the man was his backside as he disappeared into the encroaching darkness. He was set to enter the gate when he heard more speaking, this voice softer, and realized it was a bad time to approach the governor. After hearing his irritated tone, perhaps no time would be a good time. He laced his fingers between Valencia's and pulled her back onto the street.

"So the Jews think his disciples will fake his resurrection?" Val asked, baffled. "That is the most absurd thing I've ever heard." She moved in hurried steps, her legs were shorter than Lucius'.

"I knew there was more to this, Val." They immediately dropped their handhold as a group of guards moved their way on the street but continued walking back toward the barracks. "Sounds like he was teaching them that he would rise again, but that's impossible." Or was it? Sebastian had said rumors were floating around that the man had raised someone back to life. If that were true, he would be interested to see what happened in the next few days.

"Do you think it is true?"

"At this point, I don't know what is true and what is a lie anymore, except that I know nothing." Lucius paused his step and looked deep into her eyes. "I was so certain, Val. My life was planned out: serve the emperor, prove my worth, rise in the ranks, and one daydream of making you, my wife. Now all I know is that this world is so corrupt, and nothing in life makes sense right now."

"Do we make sense right now?" There was a sadness in her voice that softened him. He stopped and turned to face her.

"I love you more than life itself, Valencia." He spoke every word firmly and without breaking eye contact, searching her eyes to see if he returned his devoted love for her. He said it. He had finally told her how he felt. It was freeing, and also sad, knowing they would never be wed.

She jumped into his arms and kissed him deeply in the dark part of the alleyway, where no one could see. He let himself enjoy the moment so he could savor it when she wasn't his and more.

"Let's go somewhere more private and sulk in wine and our misery." She teased trying to lighten his mood.

He returned her smile and followed her lead, feeling now more than ever it was time to do something different. His mother would not want him serving this corrupt government. What she was unable to do through rational communication, he'd tried to do by diligence and hard work, but neither one had paid off. He could be a Legionary Commander one day, but for what? He'd never have the family he wanted with Val, and he'd have to sell his soul to do it. Pushing those thoughts aside, he wanted to just be present at this moment with Val.

Chapter Twelve

The air was dry, dust particles floating in the light that streamed in the window. Lucius had awakened as the rooster crowed. Wine had been his constant companion the past few days. He sat in the window, staring down at the street and the passersby, wondering if they had their lives figured out, if, perhaps, they knew the meaning or purpose of life. His head was foggy from drink, and the last fingers of the sun clawed at the sky, refusing to die.

It had been three days since he had beaten an innocent man and watched him be put to death. Truth and justice had been the principles upon which Lucius had lived his life. Do good and be honored; do bad and be punished. It was the foundation he had built on, and that foundation had crumbled the moment Pilate chose to sentence an innocent man to death, a death he had participated in. His confidence in everything he'd lived for was shaken to its core, and he didn't want it back.

A breeze blew in the window as the door opened, creaking on its hinges. He didn't even turn to see who it was. No one would enter his quarters without knocking, except for Val, and he was ashamed of himself for having spent the past two days in a drunken stupor. He had hidden away in his room. Now he stared at the street blankly as she approached. He could smell the hints of lavender on her skin before she even neared him.

"I'm worried about you, Lucas. It isn't like you to stay shut up like this." She spoke tenderly as leaned in the doorway.

Lucius refused to let himself look at her. It was so hard for him to let anyone see him this broken and beaten down. His eyes were heavy and his breathing was slow, the wine weighing him down. He watched a horse pull a cart on the street and noticed a small child curled up in the wagon's bed. What he wouldn't do to be a child again, to have his mother back, to feel her arms comforting him. But he wasn't a child anymore. He was a grown man, and life had dealt him a few harsh blows, wounds he wasn't sure he could come back from.

He lifted the wineskin to his lips and drank from it. His hands ached as he corked the skin and rested it back on his thigh. Bruises had appeared on his knuckles after the beating he'd dealt Barabbas in the street, and he'd hidden them from

Valencia until now. Now, he didn't care what she saw.

"Lucas, your hands." Val padded over to him and took one of his hands in hers, smoothing her thumb over the purple marks on his skin. "What happened?"

Lucius shrugged, keeping his gaze averted.

"Why aren't you talking to me? What is happening to you? You can't just sit here and drink the rest of your life." She dropped his hand to his lap and folded her arms over her chest, and from the corner of his eye, Lucius saw the hurt wash over her. "I miss you. What will make you happy again?"

Lucius felt bad for shutting her out, but he wasn't in the mood for company, and he wasn't sure when he would feel better. He turned to face her and noticed she had been crying, her red-rimmed eyes still puffy. They matched what he thought his own eyes probably looked like, though he hadn't seen himself in a mirror.

"I'm sorry." He couldn't muster much more than that, and when he spoke, he noticed how slurred his words sounded. She would be able to tell he'd had far too much to drink.

"You need to stop drinking." She swiped at the wineskin, but he pulled it away, brushing past her and uncorking it to take another large gulp. Sebastian had supplied him with plenty of wine to last his days, his way of telling him to stay away for a while. After the incident on the street, Sebastian and Tumas had been covering for him on daily sweeps of the city and night watches.

"I'm fine." He finished what little wine was left in the skin and tossed it to the floor next to the bed before tossing back the covers and crawling into it. He hadn't changed clothes in days and had been sleeping in the same outfit. He probably stank, but again, he did not care.

"You're not fine, Lucas. Look at you. Have you ever eaten?" Val sat down on the bed, her gown making swishing noises as she moved. The soft color of her cream veil made her creamy skin appear warmer than usual, or maybe she had gotten a bit of sun after having been outdoors so much the other day. Lucius didn't know, but he did enjoy the glow it created on her face.

"You're beautiful." He reached for her face, but she pushed his hand away.

"I'm worried about you."

"I'm fine," he sulked, retracting his reach and folding his fingers together. He hiccupped and then clamped his jaw shut.

"You need to sober up." She said firmly but then softened her voice. "I know what you saw was horrible. I can't imagine having to be the one to scourge a man. Just watching it was terrible. But you are stronger than this, Lucas."

The words stung. Val had no idea what he felt, and it seemed like she didn't even want to try to understand who Jesus was. They had gone and visited the tomb. The stone was extremely large and unmoveable. Val said to just wait and see but Lucius wanted more answers now. Lucius licked his lips and scraped his hand across his unshaven face.

"We murdered an innocent man. And the man Pilate pardoned ran straight out to do more harm. What is wrong with people? Why do I serve this government when this is the way they do justice?" He pushed himself up on the bed a little. "And what about the strange things that happened at

Golgotha? The clouds, and the thunder, and the earthquake. What do they mean?"

Valencia gave him a look of sympathy and turned, lying next to him with her head on his shoulder, her arm draped over his stomach. She held him tenderly without speaking for a long time. Her nearness felt right, and Lucius felt calmed by her touch.

"What do we do, Lucas? How can I help you?"

Lucius looked down at her. He had no answers. The only thing he knew he wanted to do was to take all that he had and sell it and buy passage on a ship to leave—and never come back. Build a life for him and Val away from Rome. He wanted to find answers, wherever they may be, but no one ever truly escapes Rome. Rome was everywhere. And, honestly, there was so much evil everywhere else in the world, too.

"I don't know what we will do, my love."

"I love you."

Lucas sighed, feeling sleep tugging at his eyelids. As long as Valencia was by his side, he could handle whatever came next. He decided that when he awakened, he would put on clean clothes and go speak to his commander. If Val was brave enough to commit to him even though her father would reject her, he would be brave enough to flee the guard and search out answers.

Chapter Thirteen

Early in the morning, when the faint glow of dawn had just begun to creep past the drapes, Lucius jerked awake for the second time in under three days. Noise at the door startled him. Hearing the banging, he sat up.

"Captain!" It was the voice of Tumas, and it sounded urgent. "Captain, please open the door!"

Valencia rubbed her eyes and yawned, sitting up beside Lucius.

"Go quickly to the window. Hide in the curtain." Lucius nudged her and she threw back the covers, snatching her sandals from the floor and scurrying like a mouse to hide in the drapes. They had stayed up well into the night talking, and she had fallen asleep. The effects of the wine had worn off, but he would not put her out that late hour, so she had slept in his arms.

Once Valencia was hidden, Lucius shoved his feet into his sandals and hurried to the door. Upon opening it, he noticed Tumas was out of breath, his face red from exertion and his hair damp with sweat. Panting, he leaned against the doorjamb.

"Sir, it is the tomb." His eyes were wild with urgency. " It's empty."

"What?" The blood drained from Lucius' face and he went white.

"The Jew, Jesus, the one you scourged. There is a commotion at the tomb because his body is gone. The stone has been rolled away."

"How can that be? It was under guard, and the headstone was huge." Lucius retreated into his room to grab his scabbard and armor, forgetting that he had left his breastplate and helmet lying outside days before. He searched the room for it as Tumas explained.

"The guards fell asleep, and this morning, some women came to mourn and found the tomb open and empty. They said the man appeared to one of them. Now there is a host of people around there. The people are talking and the city hasn't even woken up yet. You need to come."

Tumas's serious expression gripped Lucius. His mind raced. Had the disciples of Jesus come and stolen his body as the Jewish leaders had feared? What chaos would that cause?

"Go. I'm coming." Lucius grabbed his scabbard and tied it around his waist. As soon as Tumas was out the door and it was shut behind him, Val stepped out of her hiding place. Her wild curls framed a look of shock on her face.

"What in the world?" she exclaimed as she hopped on one foot, putting her sandal on the other.

"We have to find out." The excitement began to fill Lucius' thoughts at the idea that Jesus may very well have risen from the dead as he said he would, but that excitement was tainted by the fear that this was nothing more than a grave robbery. It wouldn't be the first time looters had rolled away a stone to steal a rich man's valuables, though no one had ever stolen a body. The idea was absurd.

When they were both ready and Lucius made sure no one would see them leaving, they left the room together. He ran down the corridor and took the stairs two at a time, Valencia hot on his heels. When his feet hit the street, he was off like a flash, pulling away from her, too worried about what scene he might find at the tombs to even remember that she was running with him. She knew where the tombs were and would understand his urgency. It was, after all, still his job as captain to maintain peace amongst the city's residents.

When he approached the place where they had laid Jesus, he saw the tomb was, in fact, open. The massive stone used to block the entrance had been rolled back, and a small crowd stood around. Everything looked peaceful, but looks could be deceiving, so Lucius drew near with caution. A group of what looked like fishermen stood next to a man Lucius knew was a zealot, and he stood next to a tax collector who worked with Valencia's father. They appeared deep in debate; one of them, a fisherman, had both hands in his hair, shocked. A few women nearby sat weeping and comforting each other.

"What is the meaning of this?" Lucius called out to the group of men.

"He is gone! Where has he been taken?" a woman wailed. "Where have you taken my Lord?"

"Hush, Joanna," one of the men spoke, his voice calm, but his face anything but. "We were gathered together, mourning the death of our teacher, when Mary came to report that he had appeared to her. He is alive." Even as he said the words, a shudder shook Lucius's body.

"But he is dead. How can a man who is dead be alive?" As he finished his sentence, Val came up behind him. He could hear her trying to catch her breath. He looked around the group with the same shock he saw mirrored on all of their faces.

"He told us this would happen. Destroy the temple and he would rebuild it in three days. Don't you remember?" another man asked, stepping forward. His bushy red beard and curly hair looked like he hadn't slept in days.

"Who was the woman? Who is this Mary?" Lucius rested his hand on the hilt of his sword as a woman stood and stepped forward. She had been comforting a few other women, but now they all watched as she recounted her tale to Lucius.

"I came to mourn here. It is our custom, sir." She was timid, keeping her eyes turned downward. Women were not often permitted to address men, and this must have been even more difficult given that she had suffered so much already. "There was an earthquake, and the stone was rolled away, and an angel appeared to me and told me my Lord has risen. And I ran to tell Peter and John" —she gestured toward the men who had spoken to Lucius— "and on the way, Jesus came to me. He told me to rejoice. He is alive. He told me to not be afraid, to tell the others to meet him in Galilee."

Lucius could hardly believe what he was hearing. This woman's account was unbelievable, yet there were dozens of people who believed her. One of the disciples spoke up and said that Jesus had appeared to them all except for Thomas. While they were eating and talking about Mary's news, he just appeared in the middle of the room. The one called Luke said, "He told us to meet him in Galilee, then he was gone."

Lucius back to Mary asked. "And you saw him?"

"Yes sir." Mary looked up and when she did, Lucius saw the sincerity in her eyes and knew she was not lying.

"Did you also see him raise the dead man?" He was fishing for more, something that would make it all make more sense, to see if it could be true. Jesus, risen?

"I am that man." A tall, slender man pushed past the others to stand in front of Lucius. "My name is Lazarus. I am from Bethany and Jesus' friend. I was dead for four days, and he raised me."

Electricity prickled Lucius's skin, and he marveled at what they were saying. The clouds that day on the hill, the earthquake, the way he'd offered his forgiveness. Lucius truly believed now that this man was the Son of True God. He backed away, speechless, as men began telling him tale after tale, things that Jesus had done, things he had taught them. Val stood beside him, soaking it all in.

The sun rose, giving enough light that Lucius could see now, and still, he was dumbstruck by the reports. *Jesus of Nazareth was alive?*

Chapter Fourteen

After prying Valencia away from the crowd of people, Lucius had dispersed them, warning them to return to their homes before Pilate discovered the commotion and sent a detachment to control them. They had gone peacefully under the watchful eyes of Lucius, Tumas, and the two guards who had nothing to say for themselves, except that they were tired and fell asleep on the job. They would answer to his commander for their lack of sobriety, but Lucius would not get involved. They'd lied so they wouldn't get in trouble with their commander when really, an angel had appeared to them and frightened them away. One of them even spoke their claim to the Jewish religious leaders, and those leaders paid the men off to keep quiet.

Lucius had gone at once to pack a bag. He made up his mind the moment Mary had looked him in the eye that he needed to go with these men to Galilee. Something within him had leaped for joy, and he had convinced Valencia to come with him. It had been a hard decision for her to leave, especially without even knowing where she was going, but she had agreed and was longing for answers, too.

Valencia sat on a large rock on the side of the road, rubbing her foot. Lucius approached her with a jug of water that Mary had bought for her.

"Do your feet hurt, my love?" he asked sweetly.

"Not terribly." She weakly smiled.

Lucius knew she was not accustomed to walking and looked at her sandals, made for the feet of a wealthy woman. Others rested nearby, the hot sun overhead baking them with its rays. Tufts of highway grass grew here and there but the landscape was mostly barren, rocky ground—hard on the feet and difficult to walk for long periods.

"We've been walking for days," she said, staring off into the distance. "What if it is for nothing?"

"I can attempt to carry you but, it will turn our two-day journey into a week. It is a long walk from Jerusalem to Galilee." Lucius laughed, lightening the mood, and sat down next to her. "And knowing the truth is more than enough to justify the trip."

She sighed but said no more.

Lucius had known the journey would not be easy for her, but he hoped it would give them the answers and the hope they both needed. Jerusalem held nothing for him anymore, not now. Even Sebastian had wished him luck on the journey, promising to take leave and visit as soon as possible. Lucius didn't know how long they would stay in Galilee, but he knew they had to go. Pilate had granted him two weeks, but Lucius had the feeling he wouldn't be coming back.

"How do you know that Jupiter has not done this great miracle? Or Apollo?" Val said, still pondering.

"I do not know, but what I do know is that I have questions, and I need answers."

Val put her sandal back on her foot and grumbled to herself about needing better footwear. Though the party they traveled with included women, Lucius knew no one and felt it would be asking too much to borrow a pair of sandals from a stranger. He took the water skin that hung from his belt and uncorked it, offering a drink to Val before having a drink himself.

One of the men journeying in the group with them stood to his feet and looked around at the tired travelers. Lucius had come to recognize him as the natural leader, the people willingly following him and placing their trust in him. He was a kind man, good-natured, and jovial, and Lucius found him to be wise and helpful the few times they'd spoken over the last few days.

"If everyone would like, we should make camp here for the night. We have two days' journey left."

The group murmured their fatigued responses, all agreeing to take a rest. The man, Simon Peter, went on to hand out directions and give tasks to each man. A few tents were erected quickly, one for men and one for women, as they had done each previous night, and within a short time, the camp was set and a fire crackled cooking a few hares. Loaves of bread were passed about, and Lucius and Val broke off a share for themselves. They sat by the fire and listened as both men and women recounted tales of the works of Jesus. Lucius marveled that the Jewish men allowed the women to speak openly, and wondered if it had anything to do with the witness of the man they called their Messiah.

Simon Peter shared a particularly interesting story that riveted Lucius. "So there we are on the way to my nephew's funeral. Jesus stops the funeral procession, right? And whispers to my sister not to cry. How was she supposed to not cry? He was her only son, and she was already a widow. He had been bitten by a viper, and the poison had killed him. Well, Jesus went right over to the boy, spoke to him, and he sat straight up."

The group erupted into applause and shouts of praise to God. Valencia looked amazed and awestruck, and Lucius couldn't help but smile as story after story revealed the love and compassion of the man Jesus. They told stories of how the Jewish leaders tested him and tried to catch him in a tangled web of confusing laws, but each time, the stories revealed that Jesus' only motive was to love his God and the people around him.

The testimony of Jesus' life deeply impacted Lucius. The roots of love began to push their way down into his bitter, hurting heart, and the more he heard of Jesus of Nazareth, the more he decided he wanted to be like him—to love like him, to forgive like him. Lucius felt at home in this community, but he also felt shame. He had been the one to beat the man, the one to escort him right up that hill to his death, and he hadn't tried to stop it at all.

So many questions stirred in his heart as he sat around that fire, but he couldn't ask them for fear that one of these people would recognize him from that day. He sat near Valencia, and even she was quiet, but he feared it was for a different reason. He wanted her to believe what they were saying was true, but each time they were alone, she would reason with him that it was this god or that. Juno had influenced Jesus to forgive the woman caught amid adultery, and Jupiter had given life back to the young centurion who had fallen sick. She had a hard time with the concept of one God.

He started to fear that this may be a turning point in their relationship, that Val might not accept who he was becoming and the direction he felt life was taking him.

That night as he lay on his borrowed bedroll, he closed his eyes and whispered his first-ever prayer. He didn't know what prayer to this Jewish God was supposed to sound like, only that his desperate longing for Valencia to be with him had stirred him to cry out.

"I pray to the Jewish God. If you are there, if you can hear me, show me, and show Valencia. Show us the way you did all those miracles and how to live. Can you forgive me for all I have done?"

He pulled his covers up over his shoulder as the night chill sunk into his bones. He shivered as he lay waiting for an answer. He didn't think a voice would boom out of the heavens. But he hoped that the stories he had heard were real. That the smiles on the faces of the people had substance behind them. Seeing their joy and peace in the unknown, he wanted that more than anything. Never had he wanted to believe anything more than he did now?

Chapter Fifteen

Arriving in Galilee, there was a lot of excitement amongst the eleven disciples. They were tired, and the majority was still somewhat skeptical, but they were here. Lucius was still hesitant to really believe that the man whose tomb was empty was really here waiting for them. For all they knew, someone really had stolen his body. Still, this is where he had told the disciples he would be. Lucius wanted to ask them the questions that burned on his heart. *Who is God? Does He care? Does He know me?* But those questions were too vulnerable to ask for himself right now. He wasn't sure he wanted to know the answers. He had done terrible, unforgivable things. How could Jesus ever forgive him? Since the night of his prayer, Valencia seemed to have a growing curiosity about this God. It made him happy that they were on this quest to find answers together.

Now, standing with those whom they'd gotten to know while journeying, Lucius felt hopeful that his search for something more would come to an end. He turned to Simon Peter and causally saluted him, offering a customary Roman thanks for allowing outsiders on this journey. He had grown fond of Peter and the other disciples.

Simon Peter swatted him away and wrapped him in a tight bear hug, squeezing as Lucius returned the embrace.

Lucius smiled. "Peter, thank you for allowing Val and me to travel with you."

Simon Peter returned his smile and patted him on the back. The other disciples were scouting out the mountain.

"Where do you think we should set camp?"

"Well, I don't know. The teacher didn't give too much direction before he disappeared." Peter laughed but Lucius could tell he was anxious. "Jesus spent much of his time there when traveling to this area. We can try camping there." Peter pointed to a spot further up the mountain that overlooked the lake.

Valencia, who had been talking with Mary a few paces away, came to him and stood waiting for him to address her. Peter acknowledged her presence and then said, "We can head there now. It is just a bit farther, only a short walk from here."

"Why are we waiting? Let's go." She smiled playfully.

Peter chuckled anxiously. "Just a bit nervous, I guess. I've made a lot of mistakes."

Peter gestured down the road that led up a hill. He began walking and others followed after him. Mary and Val fell into a natural conversation, and Lucius was left to ponder what all the things that had happened could mean. He pondered the questions, what he desired to know. Simon Peter seemed to understand that he was deep in thought—he was as well—and they walked in silence until they heard a faint voice.

The farther up the hill they got, the louder the voice got. A man spoke, drawing them in. Lucius could hear the sounds of the sea, and the breeze threatened to overwhelm the voice at times, but the more he tuned his ear to it, the clearer it became to him. A man prayed at the top of the hill.

When he finished praying, Lucius, Simon, and the women crested the top of the hill and saw who was speaking. Lucius' heart stopped, his breath catching in his throat. There, only thirty paces from him, stood the man whom he had beaten, alive.

His skin was warm, kissed by the sun. His eyes were bright, sparkling with life and energy. He smiled broadly and looked up at Lucius, making eye contact. Lucius felt frozen to the ground. He tried to move forward as Peter led him, also rejoicing, but Lucius couldn't move. He watched as the disciples had a tearful reunion with their Lord, the Son of God in the flesh, smiling and embracing his dear friends. Jesus locked eyes with

Lucius and excused himself from his emotional disciples.

"Lucas!" Jesus shouted, as if he'd know him forever. He jogged a few steps in his direction and then continued at a more respectable pace, but Lucius still remained there unmoving, his feet rooted in place. "Lucas, you came."

Jesus took Lucius in his arms and embraced him, offering a kiss on each cheek, a very intimate greeting for anyone, let alone a Roman. The bruises and wounds that should have left scars all over his face were gone, but Lucius noticed that his hands bore the marks of the nails that had punctured them. He couldn't believe what he was seeing. If he could pinch himself at that moment, he would have, just to prove that what he was experiencing was truly real.

"Jesus…" he mumbled, incredulous, eyes wide in awe. A ray of emotions surged through him in a moment: shame, awe, wonder, unworthiness. The son of God was here, hugging him as if he were his dearest friend. Lucius' eyes brimmed with tears, humbled and overwhelmed.

"Lucas, child, do not feel sorrowful for the thing you have done." Jesus' smile comforted Lucius, though he still felt the stain of guilt on his hands, despite the man's blood having been washed away long ago.

His chin dropped; he couldn't look at his loving eyes.

"Lucius, your mother would be proud of you."

Tears stung his eyes as Jesus spoke. "But I... and you..." Words would not form; his chest heaved with shame.

"Look at me." Jesus held him by his shoulders at arm's length. Lucius peered up at him through the tears. "I forgive you."

"But you were innocent... and I..."

"I forgive you, Son."

Lucius' heart burst open. The weight of years of anger drained out of him and he stood sobbing, allowing this man to speak into his heart something his mother could never have given him. Guilt that had festered inside of him melted away as Jesus repeated the words.

"I forgive you, Lucas. You didn't know."

Lucius scraped the back of his arm across his face and dried his tears. Looking into Jesus' eyes, he saw hope and love. Forgotten were all the questions he'd wanted to ask. He stood face to face with the man he had come to believe was the Son of God, who knew his name before he'd even introduced himself. He'd recognized him from that day as the man who had beaten him and offered forgiveness with a joyful smile before Lucius had even apologized.

Jesus turned over his shoulder and clapped Lucius on the back as he shouted: "Peter! Come, bring my friend Lucas some fish." Then Jesus ushered Lucius toward the group of people gathered there. Valencia, Peter and Mary followed. They all sat down together and ate, feasting on fish, bread, dates, and figs.

Something happened within Lucius' heart at that moment, and he hoped within Valencia as well. They had both seen with their own eyes the wonder that was the resurrected Christ. It truly was a miracle that Jesus sat across the fire and ate with them, talking with them and teaching them his ways. He told them, "You can see now how it is written that the Messiah suffers, rises from the dead on the third day, and then a total life-change through the forgiveness of sins is proclaimed in his name to all nations—starting from here, from Jerusalem! You're the first to hear and see it." Jesus beamed with excitement as he told them. "You're the witnesses. What comes next is very important: I am sending what my Father promised to you, so stay here in the city until he arrives, until you're equipped with power from on high."

Lucius decided in his heart that he would remain there and learn from the disciples even after Jesus departed. He would face his father and reason with him so that he could be free and live out this new life. There was so much to learn, and Jesus told them he could not stay there, that he had to return to his Father.

Jesus rose and parting said, "Go into the world. Go everywhere and announce the Message of God's good news to one and all. Whoever believes and is baptized is saved." He took his chin up to the sky and the clouds descended. Everyone present couldn't believe what they were witnessing. The clouds enveloped Jesus lifting him off the grounds. Rainbows and lights bounced off the clouds as Jesus ascended. He looked down on his disciples and gave a tender smile and waved farewell for now. The heavens opened at that moment and the glory of all the heavens and earth shone brighter than human eyes had ever seen. The disciples fell to their knees in awe and worship. Jesus was sitting at the right hand of God. Then, in an instant everything returned to ordinary. They stood there a long time, worshiping and praising God, celebrating the good news of Jesus. He had made a way for everyone to be forgiven and adopted into the family of God. They knew the mission before them and were ready to spread the good news. Lucius felt humbled that God chose him to be part of His plan.

Chapter Sixteen

"There, there!" shouted Simon Peter. His boisterous laughter charged the air with joyful, contagious electricity. Lucius balanced precariously on the boat as it wobbled back and forth. Learning how to haul in nets that were full of fish was a new adventure, but he loved it. Peter had been gracious enough for the past months to teach him everything he knew when they weren't traveling and spreading the good news of Jesus with others. Caesar had been surprised to see Lucius, but Lucius made his case and proved he was not a threat. Miraculously, Caesar granted his request to become a fisherman, leave the guard, and marry Val. Lucius smiled to himself thinking how much God had blessed him in the past few months. He felt free and overjoyed.

"I got it." Lucius hefted the net into the boat with Peter's help and Peter's brother Andrew collapsed in exhaustion once the load was hauled in. Lucius joined him, uncorking his skin and drinking deeply of the water. "Man, that is a lot of fish."

Andrew chuckled. "Should have seen the nets the day Jesus showed up onshore and told us to cast out into the deep. We almost sank the boat."

Peter cackled and added, "I think he did that on purpose just to see the looks on our faces!"

Lucius joined and corked his skin, dropping it into the boat. The small vessel bobbed on the sea as Peter took up the oars and handed one to Andrew. Together, the brothers recounted tales of following the Master as they rowed the boat back to shore. Lucius loved being part of their lives. For a few months now, he and Valencia had stayed with disciples, the travelers they'd met on the way to Galilee, and they'd taken trips with Peter here and there to teach about Jesus. The church was flourishing. It seemed daily there were hundreds, if not thousands, of men and women who learned of Jesus and chose to follow the teachings of Peter and his friends. Out of Jesus, a new religion had formed, one of love and hope, unlike any Lucius had ever known.

After seeing Jesus in the flesh, Valencia had cast down any belief that the Roman gods were real, and she'd accepted Lucius' belief in God. They'd had long talks about this new change of heart and choose to trust only Jesus and the God he taught them about. They both knew if she returned to Jerusalem and her father's house, it would mean only difficult things for her, and the end of their relationship. He'd convinced her to stay with him, and to marry him. They'd learned a lot together, however, and were ready to take the plunge. Today would be that day.

The boat went aground at the shore, and Lucius leaped out onto the sand, immediately helping the brothers care for a load of fish. They worked together as they had dozens of times already to sort the fish and repair the nets before docking the vessel. A few merchants came and bought up most of the fish, and Peter hauled the rest home with him. Lucius followed along.

"So tonight is the night, isn't it Lucas?" Peter winked at Lucius with a wry grin. "The boy becomes a man."

"Hardly," Lucius chuckled. "But tonight is the night Val and I make things the way they should have always been." A sudden seriousness gripped Lucius. "Peter, do you think Jesus would be disappointed in me that Val and I... well, that we... didn't wait until we were married?"

Peter grinned. His eyes twinkled with knowing. "Lucas, before Jesus died, when he was still on trial, I denied him three times. I was such a coward. He was being arrested and I feared for my own life, so I told the guards, the crowds that I didn't even know him. You held the weapon that brought him so much suffering and ushered him to his execution. If he can forgive those things, then I daresay he's already forgiven this small matter." Lucius nodded, relieved that Peter's wisdom exceeded his own.

The men finished their work cleaning the fish and preparing a small meal, famished after the long afternoon of fishing.

Peter gathered a few other men, friends of his who Lucius had met and grown fond of, and started toward the home of Simon the Traveler. They sang a song and played the trumpet joyfully, celebrating Lucius and Val's union. Tonight, the night of their marriage would be a time of feasting and joy. Valencia had been preparing for weeks, sewing her dress, preparing her veil, even learning more of the customs of the region. They didn't understand all the traditions, and Peter told Lucius it was okay if they didn't do it all the way others might do it; the important part was that they love one another and make their covenant before God.

When they approached Simon's home, Lucius did as he had been instructed, knocking on the door instead of entering. Simon answered and opened for him, and Lucius stepped inside to see the most beautiful woman he'd ever laid eyes on. Gone were the lavish silk gowns of wealth and luxury. Valencia wore a simple dress of linen, with small purple flowers embroidered around the hem. A veil hung across her face, hiding her beautiful smile, but Lucius knew she beamed beneath it.

"Your bride," Simon offered, gesturing toward Val.

Lucius stepped forward and carefully took the hem of the veil and folded it back, revealing her face. Tears streamed down her cheeks, though she smiled at him lovingly. Cupping both cheeks, he pulled her toward himself and brushed his lips over hers. Peter, Simon, and the men who'd accompanied him cheered and shouted, rejoicing at their love, and Lucius looked into her eyes.

"Shall we feast, my love?" he asked her, ready to celebrate with their new friends and the family who had become their own.

"Let's!" Valencia took his hand and together they rushed out into the street only to be met by dozens of more people who had joined the procession. Congratulations were shared by each person who got close enough to Lucius and Valencia to be heard. They paraded down the street to the courtyard at Andrew's house where they'd been so graciously afforded the space to feast and recognize their wedding. Wine was already flowing, and loud music welcomed them.

Lucius's heart was full. Jesus had changed everything about his life in ways he never imagined possible. His destiny had been to serve the crown. The only thing that had been certain was his duty to Caesar, and when it became obvious that he could not in good conscience continue on the path he had for his life, he'd felt like life was falling apart. Little did he know, his life was finally falling into place. He was unbelievably happy to serve such a good God who saw his brokenness, mistakes, and flaws and chose to love him despite it. He had given him salvation through Jesus Christ. Even abundantly blessed him with dear friends, a community, a purpose, and now his beautiful wife.

Valencia stared up at him as the party buzzed around them. He ignored the trays of food being passed around, the offers of wine and other strong drinks, and even the attempts to get them both to dance. All he wanted to do was get lost in her eyes and stay there forever. She'd been with him through the most trying ordeal of his life, and she'd supported him and encouraged him to follow his heart, and his heart had led him straight to their destiny, he wasn't sure where this life would take them but they would find out together.

"I love you, Val."

"I love you too, Lucius." Her smile could melt a thousand icebergs, could warm the coldest night, and it was all his to enjoy the rest of his life. Glory to God!

Made in United States
North Haven, CT
01 June 2022

19752536R00075